RESCUE MISSION!

Adapted by Steve Behling
Illustrated by Patrick Spaziante

A Random House PICTUREBACK® Book

Random House 🏠 New York

Jurassic World Franchise © 2022 Universal City Studios LLC and Amblin Entertainment, Inc. Series © 2022 DreamWorks Animation LLC. All Rights Reserved. Published in the United States by Random House Children's Books, a division of Penguin Random House LLC, 1745 Broadway, New York, NY 10019, and in Canada by Penguin Random House Canada Limited, Toronto. Pictureback, Random House, and the Random House colophon are registered trademarks of Penguin Random House LLC.

rhcbooks.com

Educators and librarians, for a variety of teaching tools, visit us at RHTeachersLibrarians.com

ISBN 978-0-593-43134-4 (trade) — ISBN 978-0-593-43135-1 (ebook)

Printed in the United States of America

10 9 8 7 6 5 4 3 2 1

Random House Children's Books supports the First Amendment and celebrates the right to read.

Darius and his friends Ben, Brooklynn, Kenji, Sammy, and Yasmina were attending Camp Cretaceous, an exclusive camp on Isla Nublar where kids could see live dinosaurs. But the dinosaurs escaped, and the kids got trapped on the island!

After several months, they finally found a way off the island. Just as they were on their way, a helicopter appeared in the sky above them.

"Attention!" said a voice from the helicopter. "Return to the dock immediately!"

The ocean looked rough, and the kids weren't sure they could make it home on the boat. So they decided to take their chances with the helicopter.

"What are you doing out here?" asked the man in the helicopter.

"Long story," Sammy said as she got in the vehicle.

Before everyone could hop aboard the helicopter, a terrifying T. rex thundered out of the jungle! The dinosaur roared and ran for the helicopter. The man jumped out, putting himself between the kids and the T. rex. The T. rex gobbled him right up!

Suddenly, the helicopter took off, with only Ben, Kenji, and Sammy aboard. They were shocked—they didn't want to leave their friends behind!

"What are you doing?" Kenji shouted at the pilot.

"Getting us out of here!" the pilot yelled. "Buckle up!"

Back on the ground, Brooklynn, Darius, and Yasmina weren't sure what to do. They couldn't fight off the T. rex. Their only option was to run! They sprinted away as the T. rex raced after them, its heavy feet shaking the jungle floor.

The kids escaped the dinosaur, but they soon encountered a second helicopter. A few men stepped out. The kids didn't recognize them. Then someone with an umbrella came out of the vehicle, and Brooklynn knew *exactly* who he was.

"Dr. Wu!"

Dr. Wu had created all the dinosaurs on the island. The kids heard him tell the other men about his mission to get a laptop from his laboratory. With the information on that computer, Dr. Wu could make even *more* frightening dinosaurs!

"We have to stop him," Brooklynn said as they hid from Dr. Wu. The kids knew they had to get to Dr. Wu's lab before he did. Maybe they could sneak in and grab the laptop before the doctor and his companions! They headed into the jungle, with Yasmina leading the way.

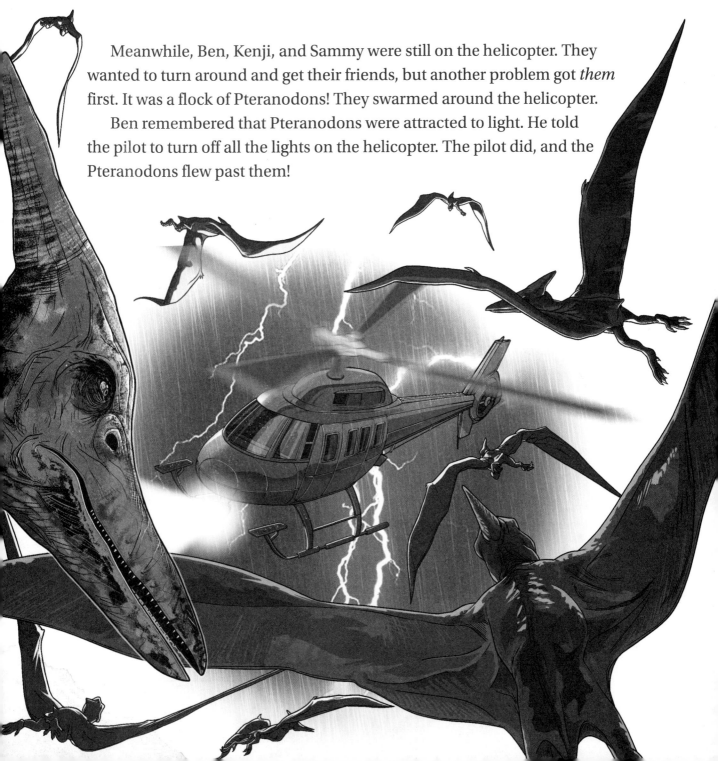

Meanwhile, Ben, Kenji, and Sammy were still on the helicopter. They wanted to turn around and get their friends, but another problem got *them* first. It was a flock of Pteranodons! They swarmed around the helicopter.

Ben remembered that Pteranodons were attracted to light. He told the pilot to turn off all the lights on the helicopter. The pilot did, and the Pteranodons flew past them!

But before they could turn back to rescue their friends, the helicopter almost flew into a Brachiosaurus! The pilot crashed the helicopter into a cluster of trees.

"Are we alive?" Kenji asked.

"I think so!" Sammy said.

Now all they had to do was get out of the tree and find their friends.

Elsewhere, Brooklynn, Darius, and Yasmina had made it to Dr. Wu's lab first! They found the laptop with his top-secret dinosaur-making information. Suddenly, they heard a sound. It was Dr. Wu and his men!

Quickly, the kids climbed inside an air vent. They watched as Dr. Wu searched his lab.

As they tried to leave the lab through the air vent, the kids were discovered by a man named Hawkes.

"Who do we have here?" Hawkes said. He reached into the vent and grabbed Brooklynn's foot.

Thinking fast, Brooklynn handed the laptop to Darius. Then Hawkes pulled Brooklynn back down the air shaft!

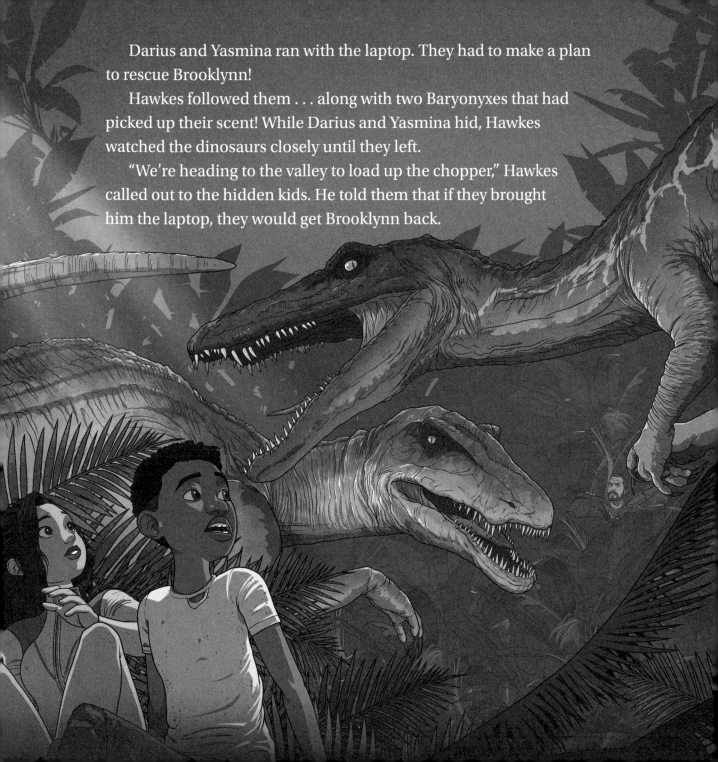

Darius and Yasmina ran with the laptop. They had to make a plan to rescue Brooklynn!

Hawkes followed them . . . along with two Baryonyxes that had picked up their scent! While Darius and Yasmina hid, Hawkes watched the dinosaurs closely until they left.

"We're heading to the valley to load up the chopper," Hawkes called out to the hidden kids. He told them that if they brought him the laptop, they would get Brooklynn back.

At last, Ben, Kenji, and Sammy had made their way back to the dock.
They thought that their friends might have gone back to the boat, too.
And a moment later, Darius and Yasmina appeared!
"Hold up," Kenji asked. "Where's Brooklynn?"
Darius and Yasmina explained the situation.

The kids returned to Camp Cretaceous. Their plan was to copy the files from Dr. Wu's laptop to Sammy's flash drive, then wipe the computer and trade the empty laptop for Brooklynn! By the time the scientist saw what they'd done, the kids would be long gone.

Ben and Darius made a model to work out the details of their plan. If everyone did what they were supposed to, it would be a success!

But Kenji wasn't so sure that the plan was such a good idea. It was taking a long time to wipe the files from the laptop. What if they didn't get to Brooklynn fast enough?

Kenji decided he couldn't wait. While the others were busy—and after Ben left to arrange for some extra help from his dinosaur friend, Bumpy—Kenji grabbed the computer and ran off.

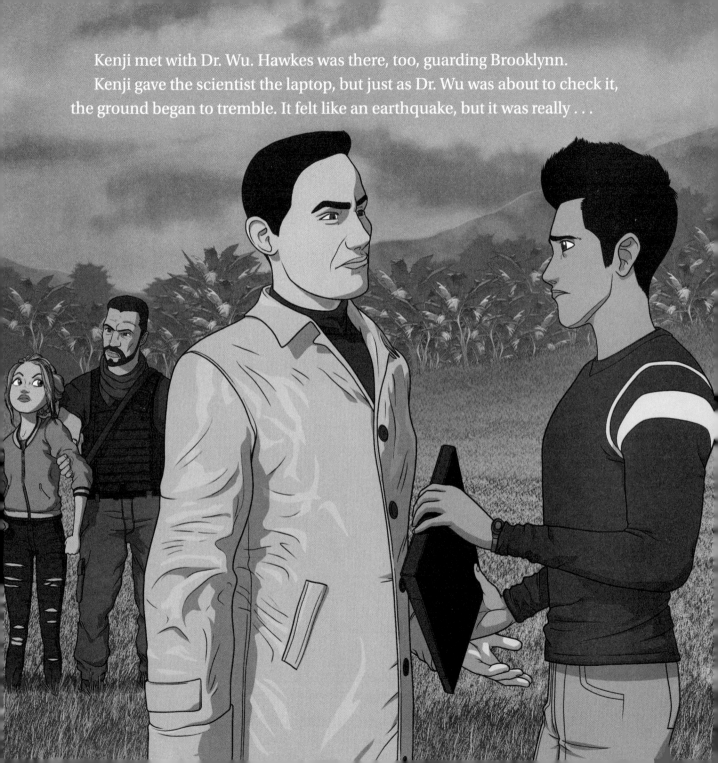

Kenji met with Dr. Wu. Hawkes was there, too, guarding Brooklynn.
Kenji gave the scientist the laptop, but just as Dr. Wu was about to check it,
the ground began to tremble. It felt like an earthquake, but it was really . . .

. . . a stampede of Ankylosauruses! Ben and Bumpy were
leading the charge. This was part of the plan!

Surprised, Dr. Wu dropped the laptop on the ground.

While Hawkes was distracted by the dinosaurs,
Brooklynn got away!

Darius went to help Brooklynn and Kenji.
Yasmina and Sammy grabbed Dr. Wu's laptop.

Avoiding the herd of dinosaurs, Sammy and Yasmina ended up back at the helicopter.

"The laptop!" Hawkes demanded. "Now!"

"Oh, you want this?" Sammy said, throwing the laptop into the path of the Ankylosaurus stampede.

CRUNCH! The laptop was destroyed!

While the kids escaped through the herd of Ankylosauruses, Dr. Wu and Hawkes took off in the helicopter. Hawkes wanted to make the kids pay, but Dr. Wu told him not to bother.

"They're not our mission," Dr. Wu said.

The kids returned to the yacht. Ben said goodbye to Bumpy, who had to stay on the island with her fellow Ankylosauruses.

"Sorry the rescue didn't go as smoothly as I'd hoped," Darius said.

"It never does," Brooklynn replied. "But somehow, it always works out!"

Darius looked at Isla Nublar as they drifted away and said, "We made it."

However, he had a feeling their adventure was not yet over.

THE END?